Praise for *A Lion is a Lion*:

"Warns a wild beast is still dangerous, however polite and friendly it seems, and even if it dances like Gene Kelly" ***Sunday Times***

"Neutralising the lion's natural threat with silliness, Dunbar gives the children of the tale the upper-hand" ***Irish Times***

"A story with playful language and rhyme that will delight families with young children" ***BookTrust***

"From start to finish, the spirits of Dr. Seuss and Maurice Sendak hover happily" ***KIrkus***

"A rousing read-aloud delight, with a trust your instincts message" ***Metro***

"Toddlers will roar (sorry) with glee" ***Literary Review***

"Children will adore following the jaunty, ever so polite Lion" ***LoveReading4Kids, Picture Book of the Month***

"A wonderfully raucous read-aloud romp" ***Baby Hampshire***

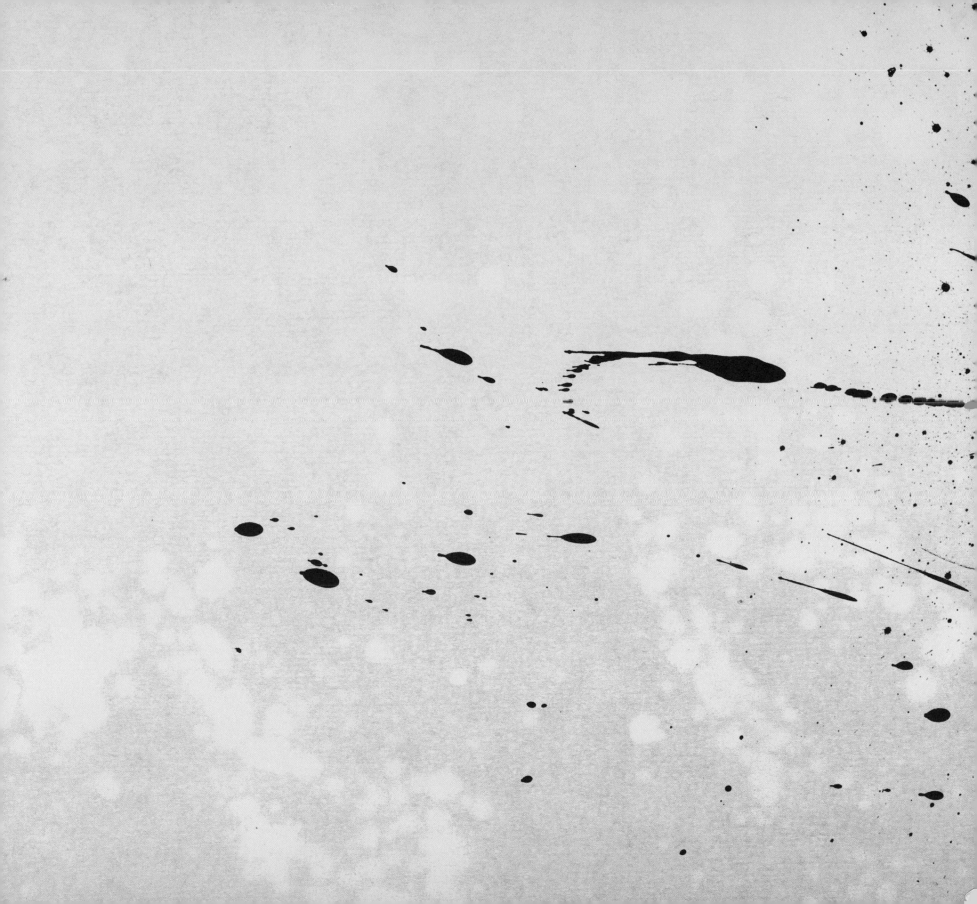

A LION

For Sonny Mac Cooper

First published 2018 by Walker Books Ltd
87 Vauxhall Walk, London SE11 5HJ

This edition published 2019

10 9 8 7 6 5 4 3 2 1

This book has been typeset in Cochin

Printed in China

British Library Cataloguing in Publication Data: a catalogue record for this book is available from the British Library

ISBN 978-1-4063-8282-2

www.walker.co.uk

IS A LION

Polly Dunbar

WALKER BOOKS
AND SUBSIDIARIES
LONDON · BOSTON · SYDNEY · AUCKLAND

This is a lion.

Fierce, isn't he?
Too fierce for you?

Well...

Is a lion
still a lion if ...

he wears a hat?

And is a lion
still a lion if ...

he carries
an umbrella,
too?

Is a lion still a lion ... if he skips down

the street singing, "Hoobie-doobie-doo"? And then ...

he hangs up his hat (his umbrella, too),

and asks, "How *IS* your Auntie Sue?"

Is a lion still a lion if ...

after the usual "How

do

you

dos?"

and "How do you don'ts!"

he says, "May I have this dance?"

And *hoobie-doobie* dances you ...

all ...

around ...

the room!

Is a lion still a lion if he says ...

"Oh, yes, lunch
would be lovely,
thank you."

And he eats all of his greens ...

and his plate, too!
'Til it's gobble,
gobble
gone!

Is a lion still a lion if ...

his eyes are bright,
and his teeth
oh-so-pearly-white
and he looks like

      he might just ...

YES!

A LION
IS A LION
IS A LION!

And now it's time to

GO! GO! GO!

OR...

Is it time to simply say ...

"No! No! No! NO!

You may NOT have pudding,
please!

Lunch was NOT lovely,
thank you!

You may NOT have this
hoobie-doobie dance.

NO WAY!

You may NOT hang up
your hat or wipe your feet.

You can take your umbrella, too!
And Never Mind Aunt Sue!

No, you may NOT
come in —

we *DO* mind if you do!"

BANG
SLAM

You
shut
that
door ...

and watch him go –
lickety-split – down the street.

PHEW!

So, please remember,
A LION IS *ALWAYS* A LION!

And do you think he'd
like to eat you, too?
('Til you're gobble,
gobble gone?)

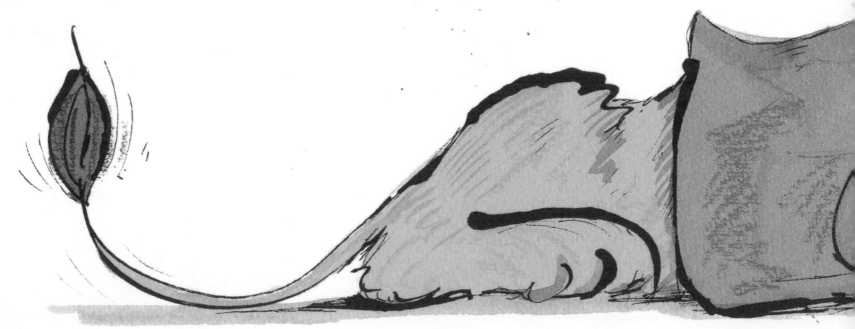

"Mmmm...
Don't mind
if I do."

No, No, No, Lion!

You may *NOT*!

NOW ... *SHOOO!*

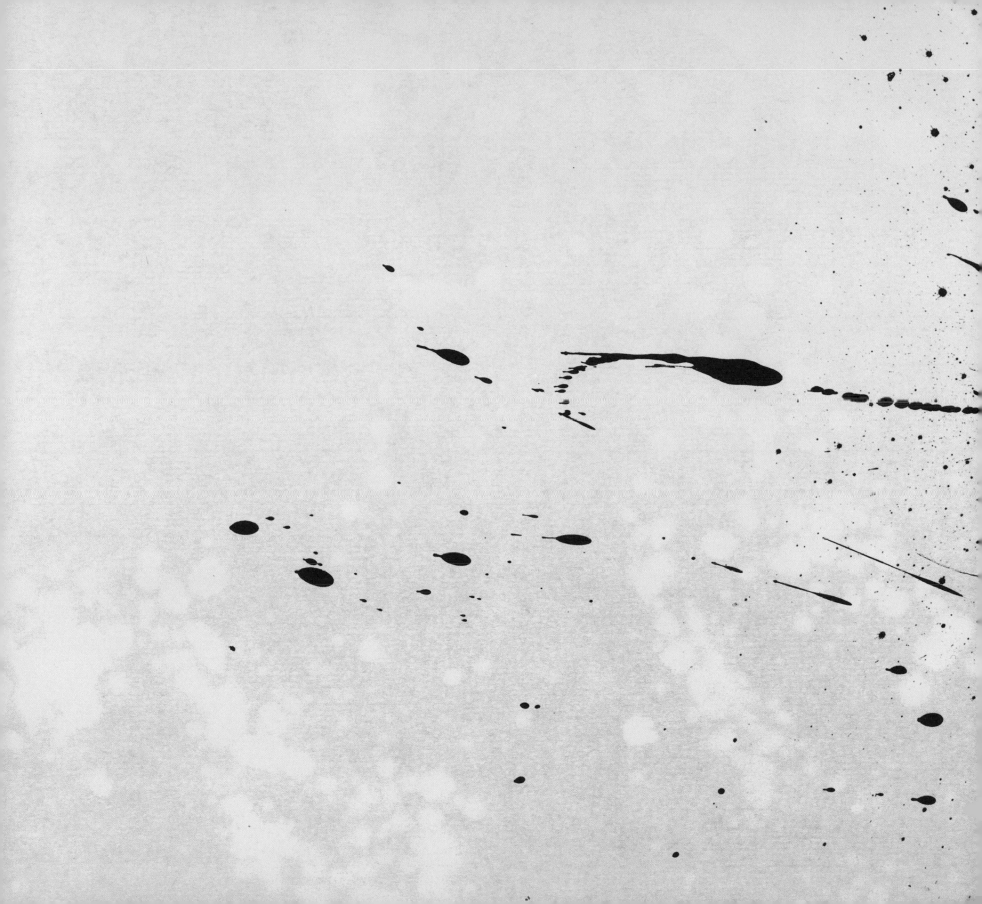

Also by Polly Dunbar:

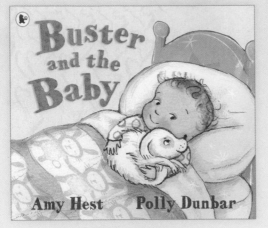

978-1-4063-8001-9

978-1-4063-7331-8

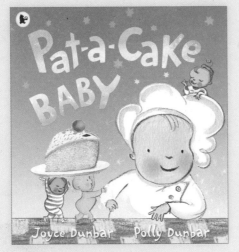

978-1-4063-6580-1

**Winner of the East Anglian
Book Award**

"Perfect for both story-time
and bedtime" *Guardian*

Winner of the BookTrust Early Years Award

**Winner of the Red House
Children's Book of the Year Award**

Winner of the Practical Pre-School Award

Winner of the UKLA Book Award

"Heart-warming … encouraging children
to remember events, read pictures
and laugh" *Sunday Times*

Available from all good booksellers 　 www.walker.co.uk